KV-105-916

Japan

Izzi Howell

W
FRANKLIN WATTS
LONDON·SYDNEY

Franklin Watts
First published in Great Britain in 2018 by The Watts Publishing Group
Copyright © The Watts Publishing Group, 2018

Produced for Franklin Watts by
White-Thomson Publishing Ltd
www.wtpub.co.uk

ISBN: 978 1 4451 5956 0
10 9 8 7 6 5 4 3 2 1

Credits
Series Editor: Izzi Howell
Series Designer: Rocket Design (East Anglia) Ltd
Designer: Clare Nicholas
Literacy Consultant: Kate Ruttle

The publisher would like to thank the following for permission to reproduce their pictures: Getty: Goryu title page and 9t, Warwick Kent 8, kanonsky 9b, SeanPavonePhoto 10 and 18, Seung Heo 12, yasuhiroamano 17r, akiyoko 20t, George_Cislariu 20b, Education Images/UIG 21; Shutterstock: Shuttertong cover, Alfonso de Tomas 4, valerylilas 5t, railway fx 5b, ESB Professional 6, Kanuman 7, artapartment 11, pawel17521 13t, TY Lim 13b, KPG_Payless 14, J. Henning Buchholz 15, pada smith 16, cowardlion 17l, Wang LiQiang 19t, Efisio Podda 19b.

Every attempt has been made to clear copyright. Should there be any inadvertent omission please apply to the publisher for rectification.

Printed in China

Franklin Watts
An imprint of
Hachette Children's Group
Part of The Watts Publishing Group
Carmelite House
50 Victoria Embankment
London EC4Y 0DZ

An Hachette UK Company
www.hachette.co.uk
www.franklinwatts.co.uk

All words in **bold** appear in the glossary on page 23.

Contents

Where is Japan?

Japan is a **country**. It is in the north east of **Asia**.

Japan is in the Pacific Ocean.
▼

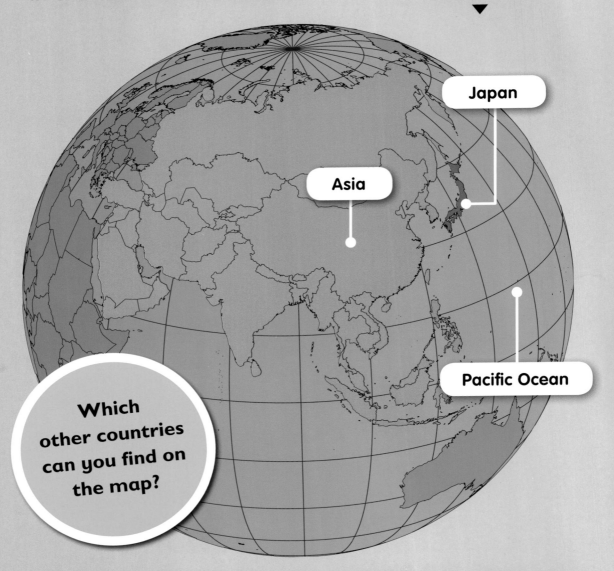

Japan

Asia

Pacific Ocean

Which other countries can you find on the map?

4

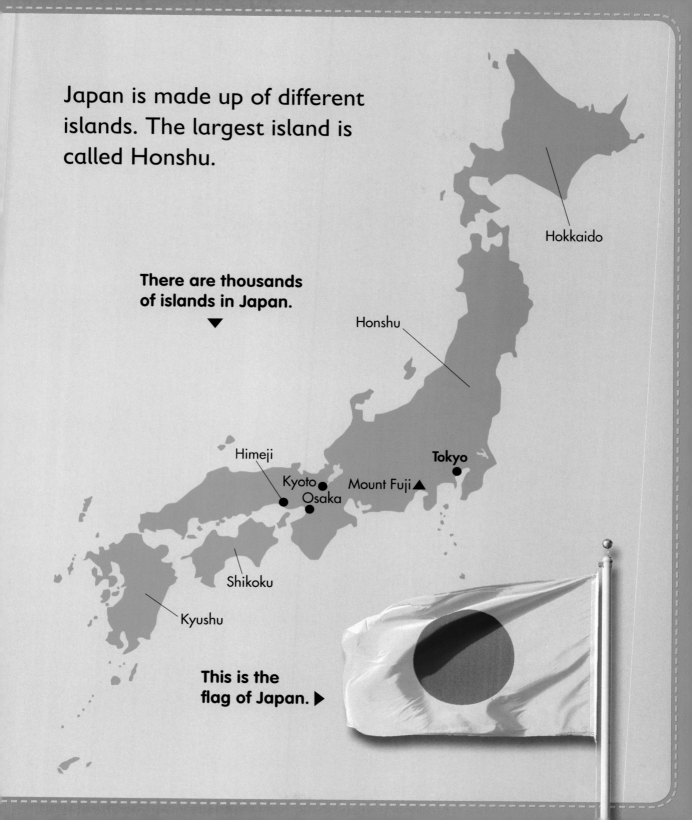

Japan is made up of different islands. The largest island is called Honshu.

Hokkaido

There are thousands of islands in Japan.
▼

Honshu

Himeji

Kyoto

Osaka

Mount Fuji ▲

Tokyo

Shikoku

Kyushu

This is the flag of Japan. ▶

Cities

Most people in Japan live in big, **modern** cities.
Tokyo is the **capital city** of Japan.

▲ **This part of Tokyo has lots of shops selling computer games.**

Some Japanese cities also have old buildings. These buildings are built from **traditional** materials, such as wood and paper.

This wooden temple in the city of Kyoto is nearly four hundred years old. ▶

What material is your home made from?

7

Countryside

Farmers plant **crops** in the countryside. They grow rice, beans and sweet potatoes.

▼ Rice plants need lots of water to grow well.

Which crops do farmers grow in your country?

There are many mountains in Japan. Some of the mountains are **volcanoes** that **erupt**. This can be dangerous for people who live nearby.

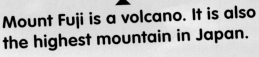

Mount Fuji is a volcano. It is also the highest mountain in Japan.

Smoke comes out of a volcano in Japan. This means it might erupt soon.

▼

Interesting places

Himeji Castle is over four hundred years old. Important Japanese **warriors** lived inside the castle. If their enemies attacked, they could keep safe inside the castle.

Himeji Castle is on a hill. ▶

The Tokyo Skytree is the tallest building in Japan. Visitors can go up the tower and look out over the city.

How would you feel if you went to the top of the Tokyo Skytree?

The Tokyo Skytree is much taller than the other buildings in Tokyo. ▶

Food

Japanese people sometimes eat with chopsticks. They hold the chopsticks between their fingers and thumb. You can pick up food by pinching the chopsticks together.

This person is eating Japanese noodles with chopsticks. ▼

chopsticks

Traditional Japanese food is healthy. People often eat rice, fish and vegetables.

Sushi is rice, vegetables and fish wrapped in seaweed. ▶

Sashimi is slices of raw fish. ▼

Would you like to eat sashimi? Why or why not?

Sport

Many people in
Japan like to watch
and play baseball.

In baseball,
a **batter** hits
the ball with
a bat. ▶

Martial arts, such as judo and karate, started in Japan. Today, many people around the world enjoy doing martial arts.

Sumo wrestling is a Japanese martial art. The wrestlers try to push each other out of a ring. ▼

Festivals

In spring, people **celebrate** the first cherry tree flowers. They come to parks to see the **blossom**.

People like to have picnics under the cherry trees.

▼

16

Shichi-go-san (seven, five, three) is a festival in November. This festival is only for children who are three, five or seven years old. They celebrate with their families.

◀ On Shichi-go-san, children wear traditional Japanese clothes.

Children eat these sweets on Shichi-go-san.
▼

Wildlife

Brown bears and snow monkeys live in the forests in the north of Japan. They have thick fur to keep them warm in the cold winter.

▼ These snow monkeys sit in **hot springs** when it's cold.

Some birds, such as owls and red-crowned cranes, live in Japan all year round. Other birds, such as sea eagles, come to Japan in the winter.

Red-crowned cranes get their name from the red feathers on their head. ▶

◀ Sea eagles catch fish off the **coast** of Japan.

Art

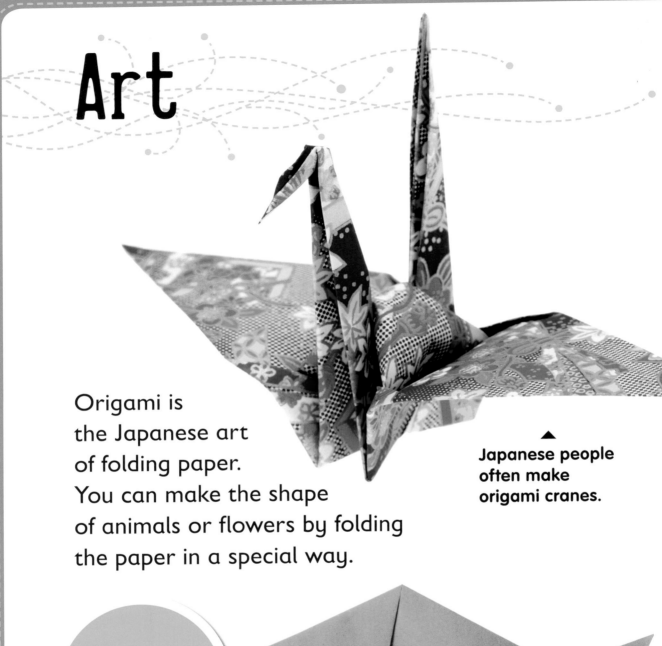

Origami is
the Japanese art
of folding paper.
You can make the shape
of animals or flowers by folding
the paper in a special way.

▲
**Japanese people
often make
origami cranes.**

**What is
this origami
animal?**

Many people read comic books in Japan. These comics are called manga. They tell stories using pictures.

People in Japanese manga comics often have big eyes and a large head.

▼

Quiz

Test how much you remember.

Check your answers on page 24.

1 What is the capital city of Japan?

2 What is the highest mountain in Japan?

3 How old is Himeji Castle?

4 Name a martial art that started in Japan.

5 When can you see cherry blossom?

6 What is the name for the Japanese art of folding paper?

Glossary

Asia – a continent that includes countries such as Japan, China and India

batter – the person who hits the ball with a bat in baseball

blossom – small tree flowers

capital city – the city where a country's government works

celebrate – to do something fun on a special day

coast – land next to the sea

country – an area of land that has its own government

crops – plants we eat that are grown by farmers

erupt – when hot, melted rock and smoke come out of a volcano

hot spring – a place where naturally hot water comes out of the ground

martial art – a traditional Asian style of fighting

modern – describes something that has been made in the past few years

raw – not cooked

temple – a building where people go to pray or worship

traditional – describes something that has been done in the same way for years

volcano – a mountain with a hole at the top, which can sometimes erupt

warrior – a soldier

Index

Answers:

1: Tokyo; 2: Mount Fuji; 3: Over 400 years old; 4: Karate, judo or sumo wrestling;
5: In spring; 6: Origami

Teaching notes:

Children who are reading Book band Purple or above should be able to enjoy this book with some independence. Other children will need more support.

Before you share the book:

- Show children different world maps and globes. Ensure they understand that blue represents sea and other colours show the land.
- Help with their understanding of the globe by pointing out countries they may have heard of.
- Talk about what they already know about Japan.

While you share the book:

- Help children to read some of the more unfamiliar words.

Talk about the questions. Encourage children to make links between their own experiences and the information in the book.

- Compare the information about Japan with where you live. What is the same? What is different?

After you have shared the book:

- Identify and discuss some familiar products/ brands that come from Japan.
- Show the children how to make some simple origami shapes.
- Find out more about the Shichi-go-san festival. How would the children like to celebrate a festival like that?
- Work through the free activity sheets at www.hachetteschools.co.uk

Countries

978 1 4451 5958 4

Where is Argentina?
Cities
Countryside
Interesting places
Food and drink
Sport
Festivals
Wildlife
People

978 1 4451 5960 7

Where is India?
Cities
Countryside
Weather
Interesting places
Food
Sport
Festivals
Wildlife

978 1 4451 5956 0

Where is Japan?
Cities
Countryside
Interesting places
Food
Sport
Festivals
Wildlife
Art

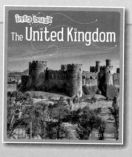

978 1 4451 5954 6

Where is the UK?
Capital cities
Countryside
Interesting places
Food and drink
Sport
Festivals
Wildlife
People

Religion

Christianity
978 1 4451 5962 1
Hinduism
978 1 4451 5964 5
Islam
978 1 4451 5968 3
Judaism
978 1 4451 5966 9

History

Neil Armstrong
978 1 4451 5948 5
Queen Elizabeth II
978 1 4451 5886 0
Queen Victoria
978 1 4451 5950 8
Tim Berners-Lee
978 1 4451 5952 2

People who help us

Doctors
978 1 4451 6493 9
Firefighters
978 1 4451 6489 2
Paramedics
978 1 4451 6495 3
Police Officers
978 1 4451 6491 5

FRANKLIN WATTS